Get that Camel!

The rose garden looked eerie in the twilight. Oliver and his friends moved slowly along the gravel path.

"Look!" Kim pointed. "Over by the gazebo."

About fifty yards away Houdini stood munching on a large rosebush.

"It's him!" whispered Oliver.

The group moved forward. They'd almost reached the gazebo when three shadowy figures appeared on the other side. "Gee-haw!" one of them shouted. He pulled out a slingshot and fired at the camel.

"Okay, boys!" shouted Rusty. "Get that camel!"

SECRET OF THE MISSING CAMEL

PAGE McBRIER

Illustrated by Blanche Sims

Troll Associates

Library of Congress Cataloging in Publication Data

McBrier, Page.
    Secret of the missing camel.

    Summary: Oliver's pet-care service faces its
greatest challenge when he is asked to watch a camel
being kept illegally in a fenced-in back yard and
it escapes into the streets.
        [1. Camels—Fiction] I. Sims, Blanche, ill.
II. Title.
PZ7.M4783Sc   1987   [Fic]   86-887
ISBN 0-8167-0816-9 (lib. bdg.)
ISBN 0-8167-0817-7 (pbk.)

10   9   8   7   6   5   4   3   2   1

SECRET
OF THE
MISSING
CAMEL

CHAPTER 1

Oliver Moffitt stepped outside and zipped up his baseball jacket. "Almost time to get out my winter coat," he said.

"Right." His friend Samantha Lawrence nodded. As the two started up Sutherland Avenue, a sudden gust of wind blew a large pile of leaves into the air. "Watch out," Sam laughed. "Pom-pom's about to blow away."

Oliver peered down at the tiny dog. Pom-pom whimpered and crawled between Oliver's legs. "I think I'd better carry him," Oliver sighed. "You know how leaves can frighten him."

Pom-pom belonged to Oliver's mother, but Oliver was responsible for walking him every day after school. Mrs. Moffitt worked at an insurance agency and never got home before six o'clock.

Oliver and Sam walked to the end of the

driveway. "Which way should we go today?" Oliver said. Pom-pom squirmed in his arms.

"Why don't we let Pom-pom decide?" suggested Sam.

Oliver undid Pom-pom's leash and set him on the ground. Pom-pom ran off toward Dewey Place. Oliver looked at the sky and shuddered. "Let's make this a quick one, Pom-pom," he called. "I think a storm is on its way."

As Pom-pom ran ahead, Sam and Oliver talked. Sam was Oliver's next-door neighbor and best friend. She was also the best athlete in her class.

"Do you think you'll be elected chairperson of the Harvest Fair?" Sam asked.

Every November, Bartlett Woods Elementary School held a Harvest Fair. There were hayrides, apple-bobbing contests, and games. The whole town was invited.

"No problem, Sam," Oliver replied. "I'm sure I'll be elected. And with all my business experience, I know I'll do a great job."

Oliver Moffitt was a pet-care expert. For several months now Oliver had run a successful pet-care business. He had watched dogs, cats, gerbils, and a monkey.

"Everyone in the class is planning to vote for you," Sam said.

"That's good," said Oliver. "I think I have most of the lower-school votes, too." Oliver was running against Rusty Jackson, the school bully. "I'm not so sure about the older kids," Oliver added. "Rusty promised every person who voted for him free bumper stickers for their bikes."

"That's bribery!" Sam said.

"Aw, he'll never win," Oliver said. "No one even likes Rusty. He'd make a terrible chairperson. Besides, it's a secret ballot. He'll never know who voted for him and who didn't." Oliver glanced at the sky again. "Where's Pom-pom?" he said.

"Here, Pom-pom," Sam called. The dog darted out from behind some bushes.

"I think it's time to be turning back," Oliver said. "I've got stuff to do at home."

Pom-pom looked at Oliver and ran off.

"Hey," Oliver called. "Where do you think you're going?"

Pom-pom wagged his tail and kept running.

"He wants us to try to catch him," Oliver sighed.

"Not again," groaned Sam. "The last time he tried this, we chased him for over an hour."

Pom-pom raced around the corner and up another street.

"This is not funny, Pom-pom," Oliver shouted. "Come back here!"

"We should never have let him off the leash," Sam panted.

A large raindrop landed on Oliver's head. "Did you feel that?" he asked. Sam nodded.

"Pom-pom," Oliver yelled, "are you crazy? It's starting to rain."

Pom-pom wagged his tail and darted up the next driveway. Sam and Oliver moaned.

"Terrific," Oliver said grimly. "*Now* look where he's headed."

Straight ahead was a tall wooden fence—tall enough to stop Oliver. But it wasn't enough for the person inside. The top of the fence had boards nailed onto it. They stuck out like a big shelf, to make sure no one could climb over. And on top of that was chain-link fencing. NO TRESPASSING signs were pasted on its side.

Sam clapped her hands together. "No, Pom-pom," she said. "You don't belong there. That's where the Fence Lady lives."

The rain started to fall in huge drops now. "Do you see him?" Oliver asked Sam.

"He's sitting over by the fence." Sam pointed.

"Great," Oliver muttered. He looked at Sam. "Well, are you coming or not?"

"I guess so," said Sam. A huge thunderclap shot through the air like a firecracker. It began to pour.

"Come on," Oliver said. "We're safest under that shelf. Besides, the Fence Lady won't be prowling around in this storm."

Pom-pom was already curled up in a ball, whimpering. "Chicken," Oliver said. He picked the dog up. "I sure hope we don't get into any trouble here."

Sam looked up and sighed. "Why would anyone want to build a fence like this?" she asked.

"I heard that the Fence Lady was once a famous actress," Oliver replied. "Everyone hounded her for autographs and stuff. She finally decided to become a hermit."

Sam's eyes widened. "Well, *I* heard that she grew up in some weird place where *everyone* lives behind big fences. She doesn't like children. Mom says she doesn't even like adults."

Oliver nodded. "The neighbors say that sometimes there are really strange noises coming from her house . . . like a baby crying."

"Maybe she keeps little children in there," Sam said. She and Oliver moved away from the fence uneasily. It was still raining heavily.

"Maybe we should make a run for it," Oliver said.

"Maybe you're right," replied Sam.

Oliver tucked Pom-pom under his baseball jacket and took off. "Let's get out of here," he said. "This place gives me the creeps."

Elections for the Harvest Fair chairperson were being held the next day during lunch. When Oliver and Sam arrived at school, they were surprised to see a group of first-graders wearing large VOTE FOR RUSTY signs. Oliver noticed his campaign manager, Josh Burns, across the parking lot. Oliver motioned him over. "Where did all these signs come from?" Oliver asked.

"Rusty gave them free bumper stickers," Josh replied.

Oliver watched as several VOTE FOR RUSTY signs marched by. "Do you really think they'll vote for him?" he asked.

"Who knows?" Josh shrugged. "First-graders

are likely to do anything. Who knows how little kids think?"

"If Rusty can get the lower-school votes, he may have a chance of winning," said Sam. She called one of the first-graders over. "Do you know how to read?" Sam asked. The little boy shook his head.

Sam smiled and got a felt-tipped marker out of her book bag. She crossed out Rusty's name and wrote OLIVER instead. "When it's time to vote, tell all your friends to copy down the name of the person on your sign," Sam explained. The boy nodded. "Good," said Sam. "Now, why don't you bring the rest of your friends over here? We want to fix the spelling on their signs, too."

For the rest of the morning Oliver was too excited to think about school. When the bell rang for lunch, he threw his books into his desk and raced for the door.

The lunchroom was already packed. Oliver noticed Rusty and his friends standing by the ballot box. Rusty was holding a stack of shiny bumper stickers.

"Maybe we should have campaigned harder," Oliver told Josh.

"Don't worry," Josh said. "As long as Rusty doesn't see the signs, we're okay."

Jennifer Hayes ran over. "Look at this cute bumper sticker Rusty gave me," she said. Jennifer was in Oliver's class.

"Does that mean you're voting for him?" Oliver said. "I thought you were voting for me."

"It'll look nice on my bulletin board," Jennifer replied. "Besides, it's my favorite color—purple."

"Great," Oliver muttered to Josh. Just then Oliver felt someone grab the back of his collar.

"How's it going, pal?" said Rusty.

Oliver squirmed. "You're choking me," he said.

Rusty tightened his grip. "Did you happen to notice my VOTE FOR RUSTY signs?" he said. "It looks like someone was busy with a red marker."

Oliver twisted his shoulder. "No one I know," he said. He noticed that Josh had disappeared.

Rusty let go of Oliver's collar. "I hope not," Rusty said. "I don't like people messing with my private property." He flashed a sinister grin and walked off.

Josh reappeared. "What happened?" he asked.

Oliver looked at Josh and shrugged. "I don't know, Josh," he said. "Maybe we underestimated Rusty."

At five minutes to three Mr. Thompson, the school principal, made the announcement on the loudspeaker. "Attention, boys and girls," he said. "I have the results of the Harvest Fair election. First, I want to thank both boys for their willingness to put in the hard work this job requires." Oliver smiled nervously and looked around the classroom. "It was a very close race," Mr. Thompson continued, "but the winner is Oliver Moffitt."

Oliver breathed a sigh of relief. His classmates cheered loudly. The bell rang, and school was dismissed. Josh, Matthew, and Sam ran over to Oliver's desk to congratulate him.

"Good work," said Sam.

"Thanks," Oliver replied. "I couldn't have done it without you."

That night Oliver sat at his desk and started to make plans. He was concentrating so hard that he didn't hear the phone ring.

"Are you going to answer that or not?" Mrs. Moffitt called from the kitchen.

Oliver jumped and picked up the phone. "Hello," he answered. "Pet-care service."

"I saw your ad in the *Citizen*," said a woman's voice.

Several months earlier Oliver had run a free advertisement in the local paper.

"Yes?" said Oliver politely.

There was a long pause on the other end.

"I'd like to arrange an appointment," the woman said.

"Okay," Oliver replied. "What kind of pet do you have?"

"When is a convenient time for you?" the woman continued.

"How about tomorrow after school?" Oliver said.

"I'll see you at four o'clock. Four fifty-three

Vanderbilt." Before Oliver could respond, she hung up the phone.

"Hmm," said Oliver. "That was weird."

The next day Oliver chose Josh, Sam, and Matthew Farley for the Harvest Fair committee. When Ms. Callahan reminded Oliver that there weren't enough girls on the committee, he also appointed Jennifer Hayes and Kim Williams.

During lunch the committee held its first meeting. "I'd like to have a rock band for the entertainment this year," Jennifer said.

"What was wrong with the magician we had last year?" Matthew asked.

"Ugh," Jennifer replied. "Boring."

"That magician was great!" Josh said. "Remember when he sawed that third-grader in half?"

"Big deal," said Jennifer. "It's all done with mirrors. Besides, if we had a rock band, people could dance." Jennifer's best friend, Kim, nodded her head in agreement.

Josh and Matthew made faces.

"Why don't we come back to the entertainment later?" Oliver suggested. "Let's talk about the food instead."

"How about *punch*?"

Oliver felt someone hit him on the back. He turned around angrily. "Why did you hit me, Rusty?" he said.

"Punch," said Rusty. "Get it?" He punched Oliver again.

"This is a private committee meeting, Rusty," said Sam.

"I'm not bothering anyone," Rusty replied. He snatched a piece of paper from the table. "What's this?" he read. "Entertainment ideas . . . a rock band." Rusty looked up. "Great idea," he said.

"You really think so?" Jennifer smiled.

Oliver grabbed the piece of paper.

"This is a *private* meeting, Rusty," he said. "You're not invited."

Rusty laughed and turned away. "What do I care?" he said. "I don't even *want* to come to the Harvest Fair now. Not with *you* creeps running it."

Oliver shook his head and watched Rusty walk off. "Now, where were we?" he said.

After school Oliver was so busy making plans that he nearly forgot his appointment. When he realized the time, Oliver jumped up from his seat. "Gotta go, guys," he said. "I have a four o'clock meeting with a new customer on Vanderbilt." Oliver ran out to his bike and hopped on. A few minutes later he was speeding up Vanderbilt. Oliver slowed down to look at the house numbers. "Four forty-nine, four fifty-one, four fifty-three," he read.

Oliver threw on the brakes and gasped. "This can't be it," he said. Oliver stared at the mailbox. "I must have the wrong address," he muttered. Just as he turned his bike toward home, the Fence Lady stuck her head out the gate. She was wearing a strange robe that hung to the ground.

"Mr. Moffitt?" she said.

Oliver nodded slowly. His heart started to pound.

"Come in," she said. "I've been expecting you."

Oliver's thoughts raced as he walked up the driveway. It wasn't too late to turn back. He could pretend to get sick. Or he could tell the Fence Lady he wasn't accepting new customers. Or he could *really* chicken out and just make a run for it.

Oliver thought some more. He had never in his life heard of anyone who had been inside the Fence Lady's house. Oliver would be the only one ever to be allowed inside. Wait till his friends heard about this! Oliver took a deep breath and entered.

The living room was dark. Oriental rugs and colorful cushions were scattered across the floor. Several decorated swords and daggers hung from one wall. A beaded curtain covered the doorway.

"Wow," said Oliver. "It looks like Lawrence of Arabia lives here."

The Fence Lady smiled. "Please remove your shoes and have a seat on one of the cushions," she said. "Would you care for some tea?"

"Yes, please," replied Oliver. He had had tea only once before in his life. He hoped the Fence Lady wasn't planning to poison him.

The Fence Lady nodded and disappeared behind the beaded curtain.

Oliver was really curious now. What sort of pet did this strange lady have? He examined the room carefully. Over in one corner was a huge covered wicker basket with a tightly sealed lid. On top of it was a musical instrument that looked something like a clarinet.

Oliver grinned. "That's it!" he said softly. "She's a snake charmer!"

Oliver felt much better. He knew all about caring for snakes. Kim's brother, Parnell, had a six-foot boa constrictor named Squeeze Me.

The Fence Lady returned. On a funny-looking bronze tray she carried a tiny teapot and two tiny cups. She placed the tray on the floor and knelt beside it.

"My name is Arabella Church," she began. "I've lived most of my life in North Africa, which is why my house looks like it belongs to Lawrence of Arabia."

"There are lots of interesting snakes in North Africa," Oliver said, glancing toward the wicker basket.

Arabella arched her eyebrows. "I suppose," she replied. She handed Oliver a teacup. "How long have you had your business?" she asked.

"A long time," Oliver replied. "Since last summer."

The Fence Lady nodded thoughtfully.

"But I've been interested in animals all my life," Oliver added quickly.

"And what sort of pets do you normally watch?" asked Arabella.

"Mostly dogs, cats, birds . . . the usual," Oliver replied. "But I really enjoy taking care of snakes, too."

"I see," said Arabella.

Oliver thought about what his mother would say if he brought home a snake. He said, "My mother really hates mice and snakes, though."

"So do I." Arabella shuddered.

"But I thought that's what you had!" Oliver said.

The Fence Lady put down her teacup. "Whatever gave you that idea?" she said sweetly.

Oliver began to wonder why he was sitting in the Fence Lady's living room.

"Can you keep a secret?" asked Arabella.

"Of course," said Oliver.

The Fence Lady thought a bit. Then she stood up. "Let me show you something." She led Oliver over to the corner of the room and pointed at the floor. "Have you ever seen one of these?" she asked.

"It looks like a small red stool," Oliver replied.

"What do you suppose it's used for?" Arabella asked.

Oliver knelt down beside the small stool. A long leather cushion sat on top of four wooden legs. Sticking up from the front was a shiny brass knob. "It looks like some sort of weird saddle," Oliver said.

"Good," said Arabella. "You're a bright boy. Polite, too. I think you're trustworthy enough to keep my secret." She led Oliver through the kitchen and out the back door.

"Oliver," she said, "I'd like you to meet Houdini."

Oliver rubbed his eyes and gasped. "I don't believe it!" he said. "*This* is your pet?"

CHAPTER 2

"**W**hat do you know about camels?" asked Arabella.

"Not a lot," Oliver admitted. "This is the first one I've ever met."

"Camels are intelligent, playful, and patient," said Arabella. "Each has its own personality." Arabella paused. "But they can also be quite dangerous," she said. "An angry camel will bite, spit, and kick."

Oliver nodded solemnly.

"I have to leave town for about three weeks," Arabella said.

"Three weeks?" Oliver said.

"Don't worry," she continued, "I won't leave Houdini with you for that long. Besides, he's usually very well-behaved. I just need you to make sure he's properly fed and watered until my cousin Henry arrives. He should arrive here from Australia three days after I leave."

Three days didn't seem like such a long time to Oliver. He glanced over at Houdini, who was happily munching on a thorn bush. "You've got yourself a deal," he said.

Arabella reached into her pocket and pulled out a handful of jellybeans. Houdini immediately lifted his head and walked over.

"Camels love treats," Arabella said. Houdini stretched out his neck and nuzzled Arabella's hand. His large brown eyes had thick, curly lashes. On his front knees and chest were leathery-looking pads.

"I thought camels were bigger than this," Oliver said.

"Houdini's still a baby," Arabella replied. "He's just a year old. He'll grow another two feet before he's full-sized."

Houdini gave Oliver a curious stare.

"What else does he eat?" Oliver asked.

Arabella led Oliver over to the garage. Inside, a stall had been built. Over in the corner were two bales of hay and a barrel of oats. "Every morning and evening I feed him some hay and a handful of grain. As a treat he gets a chopped-up carrot or apple."

Houdini leaned down and stuck his nose into Arabella's pocket. "No more jellybeans today," she said, pushing him away. Houdini groaned.

"Why did he do that?" asked Oliver.

"Camels groan if they're unhappy," Arabella

North Hills Baptist Church and Christian School

laughed. "But he knows he's not allowed too many jellybeans. They're bad for his teeth."

"Right," said Oliver. He looked around the garage. "How often does he need water?"

"Contrary to what most people think, camels need lots of water," said Arabella. "I give him three or four buckets a day, although he could go several days without it if he had to."

Arabella spent a long time explaining Houdini's routine and showing Oliver around the back yard. Oliver was to stop by twice a day. "I'm low on supplies," Arabella said, "but Cousin Henry will arrange for more when he arrives. He's always owned a camel or two himself."

"How did you get Houdini?" Oliver asked. "I thought it was illegal to keep a camel as a house pet."

Arabella sighed. "It's a long story," she said. "When I moved here from North Africa, I managed to sneak Houdini's mother, Genie, into the country. Unfortunately the authorities found out and insisted she be returned. What they didn't know was that she was pregnant. After Houdini was born, I sent Genie back and kept the baby. I bottle-fed him myself."

Arabella looked at Oliver sternly. "You mustn't ever tell anyone about Houdini," she said. "He's very special to me, and I couldn't bear to have anything happen to him."

"Don't worry," Oliver said. "Your secret is safe with Oliver Moffitt."

*   *   *

Oliver's duties began the following Monday. Over the weekend Oliver had gotten several books on camels from the library. He learned that Houdini was a dromedary, or one-humped camel. He was also surprised to find that thousands of years ago camels were abundant in North America.

Oliver was up and out of the house before his mother and Pom-pom awoke. He left his mother a note on the kitchen table:

Dear Mom,

I had to go to a Harvest Fair committee meeting.
See you tonight.

O.M., Chairperson

Houdini was still asleep when Oliver unlocked the gate and let himself in. Oliver watched as Houdini stood up by straightening first his back legs and then his front. Houdini stamped his feet impatiently until Oliver fed him his hay and oats and refilled his water tub. Then Oliver opened the garage door so that Houdini could wander around the yard. "Nice camel," he said, gently patting Houdini on the neck. Houdini didn't look up from his breakfast.

Oliver slipped out of the yard. He carefully bolted the top lock on the gate and then glanced around nervously. He had a feeling he wasn't alone.

Oliver ducked behind a bush and watched

several cars drive by. After the traffic was gone, he finished locking the gate.

"Fancy meeting you here," said a familiar voice.

Oliver spun around. "Rusty! Where'd you come from?" he said. Oliver stuffed the keys into his back pocket.

Rusty pulled a toothpick out of his mouth. "Just hanging around," he replied. "How about you?"

"The same," Oliver shrugged.

Rusty looked at the gate. "Where'd you get the keys?" he asked.

Oliver's heart began to pound. "What keys?" he replied.

Rusty grabbed him by the collar. "I saw you lock up the gate," he said. "Don't lie."

"Ouch, leave me alone," Oliver said. "I was just feeding the lady's cat."

Rusty snickered and let go of Oliver's shirt. "Cat, huh?" he snorted. "You mean to tell me there's a giant fence here to protect a little cat?"

Oliver straightened out his collar. "Look, Rusty, I have to go," he said. "I don't want to be late for school." He hopped on his bike and quickly pedaled away.

Oliver managed to avoid Rusty for the rest of the day. When the three o'clock bell rang, Oliver was the first one out the door. He made extra sure that no one followed him from the parking lot.

Oliver pulled up to Arabella's and carefully let himself into the back yard. Houdini was busy rolling in the dirt. "Hi, Houdini," Oliver called. Houdini ran over and playfully grabbed at Oliver's back pocket.

"Hey, what do you think you're doing?" Oliver said.

Houdini gave another snort and kicked his heels.

Oliver reached into his pocket and pulled out a candy bar. "Is this what you're looking for?" he asked.

Houdini craned his neck forward.

"Sorry," said Oliver, sticking the candy bar back into his pocket. "Candy is not good for camels."

Oliver walked over to the garage and bent down to get a scoop of oats. He felt another tug on his pocket. "No, Houdini," said Oliver. Before Oliver could reach back, Houdini lifted the candy bar high over Oliver's head. Houdini ran out into the yard.

"Bad camel," said Oliver. "You give that back."

Houdini looked at Oliver and swallowed.

Oliver shook his head and laughed. "I knew you had a sweet tooth," he said, "but Arabella didn't tell me you were a thief."

Houdini playfully flicked his tail and ran off.

The next two days went by quickly. Each morning and each evening Oliver faithfully checked on Houdini. During school he was busy with plans for the Harvest Fair.

On Wednesday evening Oliver stopped by Arabella's for the last time. Cousin Henry was due to arrive the next day. Oliver looked around. He was glad he hadn't run into Rusty again.

Houdini chewed his cud and nuzzled his head on Oliver's shoulder. He'd already found the jellybeans Oliver had hidden for him in his book bag. "Maybe I'll come by this weekend," Oliver said. "Would you like that?"

Houdini flicked his tail and stared at Oliver with his big brown eyes. "Good camel," said Oliver. He made sure the gate was securely locked and headed for home.

Friday was cold and gray. "Did you know it may actually *snow* this afternoon?" Mrs. Moffitt said at breakfast.

Oliver shook his head and thought about Houdini. He remembered reading that camels can't stand wet weather. Their hooves slip easily. Also, they can develop arthritis. Maybe today would be a good day for a visit.

"I'll be home late this afternoon," Oliver said suddenly. "I've got some things to do after school."

Mrs. Moffitt smiled. "Harvest Fair committee, right?" she said.

"Right," said Oliver.

As soon as the last bell rang, Oliver headed for Arabella's. Thick black storm clouds had started to gather in the sky. Oliver hoped Houdini was safe inside the garage.

Oliver unlocked the gate. He was glad to see the garage door closed. "Hello-o-o," Oliver called. "Anyone home?"

Oliver could hear Houdini impatiently stamp his feet.

"Hello-o-o," Oliver called again. The back yard was quiet. "That's strange," Oliver thought. "It looks like no one's been here."

He walked over to the garage window and peered in. Houdini's feed bucket and watering tub were empty. Houdini stared at Oliver and then anxiously threw his head up and down.

"Uh-oh," said Oliver. "I was right!" He ran over and opened the door.

Houdini immediately began to howl. Oliver tossed him a section of hay and then filled the water tub to the top. "Drink up," Oliver said.

Houdini drank and drank.

Oliver filled the tub a second time. Houdini kept on drinking.

"Wow," said Oliver, "you must have really been thirsty!"

In the far corner of the garage Oliver examined the supplies. Houdini had eaten all the oats, and only one bale of hay was left.

Oliver sat down and sighed. "What now?" he thought. He couldn't leave Houdini alone. He would have to take care of him until Cousin Henry or Arabella showed up.

Oliver reached into his back pocket and pulled out a candy bar. Houdini stretched his neck.

Oliver split the candy bar in half. "Don't worry, Houdini," he said. "Oliver Moffitt would never desert a pet."

CHAPTER
3

After Oliver made sure that Houdini was comfortable, he went inside the house. On a low table by the front door was an unopened envelope that said, "Cousin Henry." In the guest room a set of clean towels sat neatly on the bed. There were no dirty dishes in the kitchen sink. "How weird," thought Oliver. "Where could Cousin Henry be?"

That night Oliver sat in his room and wrote out a shopping list:

    2 bales hay
    1 barrel oats
    1 bag carrots
    1 bag apples
    1 bag jellybeans

The last three items were no problem. He could pick them up at the Quick Shoppe. But where would he find oats and hay?

Mrs. Moffitt stuck her head inside the door. "Don't forget about tomorrow," she said.

Oliver looked puzzled.

"You promised to help me give Pom-pom a bath," she said.

"Oh, right," Oliver replied. "First thing in the morning." He looked out the window. The snow was still falling lightly. Houdini's yard would need to be shoveled tomorrow before it got too icy. Also, Josh was coming over in the afternoon to help Oliver figure out the Harvest Fair budget.

Oliver shook his head and sighed. How was he ever going to get it all done?

Oliver was up early the next morning. The first thing he did was look out the window. "Not bad," he said. "Only one inch of snow. That shouldn't be too hard to shovel."

Oliver ran to the bathroom and filled the tub with lukewarm water. He threw in a little Puppy Potion Bubble Bath. "Here, Pom-pom," he called. "Bath time!"

There was no answer.

Oliver tiptoed into his mother's room. She and Pom-pom were still asleep. "Rise and shine," said Oliver.

Mrs. Moffitt rolled over and opened one eye. "Oliver!" she said. "It's so early!"

"Everybody up," Oliver said. "Pom-pom, your bath is ready."

Pom-pom hopped onto Mrs. Moffitt's bed and crawled under the covers.

Mrs. Moffitt yawned. "Oliver, why don't you go fix yourself some breakfast first? It's only six o'clock."

Oliver left the room with a loud sigh. He hoped Houdini was all right. He wandered down to the kitchen and opened the cereal cabinet. A box of oatmeal caught his eye. Oliver suddenly had a great idea. "If camels eat oats, why won't they eat oatmeal?" he thought.

Oliver grabbed the largest pot he could find. He filled it almost to the top with water. After the water started to boil, he dumped in the entire box of oatmeal.

A few minutes later Oliver's mother called from upstairs. "How about giving Pom-pom that bath now?" she said.

"No problem, Mom," Oliver called. He ran back to the bathroom and got the bath water ready again. While Oliver scrubbed, Mrs. Moffitt held Pom-pom still.

"Oliver, what's that noise?" Mrs. Moffitt said suddenly. "It sounds like it's coming from the kitchen."

Oliver stopped scrubbing and listened.

"Something is spilling over," said Mrs. Moffitt.

"Uh-oh," said Oliver. "I forgot the oatmeal." He ran quickly downstairs. The oatmeal had boiled over and covered the kitchen floor. Everything was a gooey mess.

"What happened?" Mrs. Moffitt gasped as she entered the kitchen.

"I was just making myself a little breakfast, Mom," said Oliver.

It took Oliver all morning to clean up. The oatmeal stuck to everything.

By the time Oliver stopped by the Quick Shoppe and got to Arabella's, it was already lunchtime, and still no Cousin Henry.

Oliver fed Houdini an apple, a section of hay, three jellybeans, and all the oatmeal he scraped off the kitchen floor. Then he carefully shoveled the yard and cleaned out Houdini's stall.

Oliver looked at his watch. "Oh, no!" he said. "I was supposed to meet Josh at my house an hour ago."

Oliver ran home as fast as he could. "Where have you been?" asked Mrs. Moffitt. "Josh was here looking for you."

"I had some errands to do," Oliver answered. "Did Josh go home?"

"He said to tell you he won't be around for the rest of the weekend. He's going to his grandmother's."

"Great," mumbled Oliver. "Now I won't be able to finish the budget."

Oliver went to his room to think. Life was getting complicated. He drummed his pencil on the desk. "Where am I going to find hay and oats?" he thought. "I know!" Oliver said. "The Harvest Fair always has a hayride. I'll just order extra hay and have it delivered early."

Oliver called Shamrock Stables. "Mr. O'Brien?"

39

said Oliver. "This is Oliver Moffitt, chairperson of the Bartlett Woods Harvest Fair."

"And would you be calling to order the hayride?" boomed Mr. O'Brien.

"That's right," said Oliver. "Only this year we'd like the hay delivered a little early. We want to set up a harvest display in the lobby."

"Good idea," said Mr. O'Brien. "When would you like it delivered?"

"How about tomorrow?" said Oliver.

"Don't normally work on Sunday," Mr. O'Brien replied.

"What if I met you at school and helped you unload?" said Oliver.

"I suppose I could do that," said Mr. O'Brien.

"I'll be at the playground tomorrow at ten o'clock," Oliver said. "Thanks a lot." He breathed a sigh of relief and hung up.

Mr. O'Brien showed up the next day right on time. He and Oliver unloaded six bales of hay near the fifth-grade classroom and covered them with a large gray tarp.

Mr. O'Brien shook Oliver's hand. "Thank you, Mr. Moffitt," he said. "Molly and I will be here with the wagon next Saturday." He turned to go.

Oliver had another idea. "Mr. O'Brien," he said, "you wouldn't happen to have any oats, would you?"

Mr. O'Brien put his hands on his hips. "Now, why would you be wanting oats?" He smiled.

"I thought they'd look nice with the display," Oliver said quickly. "Next to the harvest basket."

Mr. O'Brien opened the back of his truck and dug around for a few minutes. He handed Oliver a bucket. "Here you are, son," he said. "I don't think Molly will mind my giving you a bucket of her oats. Just don't try making them into oatmeal."

"No, sir," said Oliver. "I'd never do that."

Oliver waited until Mr. O'Brien was out of sight and then he carefully opened the tarp. He took out one bale of hay. Then he sat the bucket of oats on top and gingerly carried them across the school yard.

It took a long time to reach Arabella's. At the gate Oliver threw down the hay and oats and took out his keys. The lock on the gate was dangling open.

"Hmm. I know I locked that," Oliver thought. He quickly pushed the bale of hay and the bucket of oats into the yard. "Cousin Henry?" he called. "Is that you?"

There was no answer. Oliver closed the gate and tried again. "Yoo-hoo, Cousin Henry," he called. Oliver heard Houdini kick the garage door.

Suddenly Oliver felt someone grab him from behind and put a hand over his mouth. Oliver struggled to get free. "Stop it," he said. "Leave me alone."

"Sure, pal," Rusty grinned. "As soon as you tell me what's going on."

Oliver tried to turn around, but Rusty held

41

his arm in a tight hammerlock. "Start talking," Rusty said.

"How did you get in here?" Oliver demanded.

Rusty tightened his grip. "I thought I was the one asking the questions."

"Ouch," said Oliver. "Let go."

"Not until you tell me about Cousin Henry and why you dragged that bale of hay from the school yard."

Oliver tightened his lips.

Inside the garage Houdini groaned.

"Ah-ha!" said Rusty. He shoved Oliver over to the garage door. "Okay, Moffitt," he said, "open the door."

"What?" said Oliver weakly.

"You heard me," Rusty said. "Now."

With a sigh Oliver opened the door. Houdini galloped into the yard.

"Wow!" cried Rusty. "It's a camel!" He let go of Oliver's arm and slapped his thigh. "Gee-haw!" Rusty yelled. "Giddy-up, Cousin Henry."

"His name is Houdini," said Oliver. Rusty wasn't listening.

Houdini ran over and playfully butted his head against Rusty's shoulder. "Hey, call off your camel," Rusty said. "This is a new leather jacket."

Houdini knocked Rusty's shoulder a second time.

"I said watch it, Henry!" yelled Rusty. With one sharp motion he kicked Houdini's back leg.

"I wouldn't do that if I were you," Oliver said.

"He needs to know who's boss," Rusty said. He slapped Houdini on the nose.

Houdini's eyes flashed. He kicked Rusty in the arm.

"Knock it off," screamed Rusty. He angrily raised a fist.

Houdini snorted and lifted his head. From his mouth came a disgustingly large green wad of saliva. It landed on Rusty's jacket and oozed down his sleeve.

Rusty hopped up and down and waved his arms. "Get away from me, you crazy animal," he shrieked.

But Houdini wasn't finished. With a roar he bared his teeth and reared up on his hind legs.

"Help," screamed Rusty. "Get me out of here." He ran for the gate. "I'm not finished with you, Moffitt," he growled over his shoulder. "You'll see."

Oliver took a deep breath and leaned against the garage door. He'd never seen Houdini so angry. Even worse, Rusty was sure to tell everyone about the camel. Arabella's secret was ruined. Houdini would be sent off to North Africa. And it was all Oliver's fault!

The next day at school was a disaster. "Oliver," said Ms. Callahan, "may we see your Harvest Fair budget?"

Oliver looked down at his desk and shook his head. "It's not quite ready," he said. He could feel everyone in the class looking at him.

44

"I thought you said you'd finish it over the weekend," said Ms. Callahan.

"I didn't have time," Oliver mumbled.

"Maybe it would help if you appointed a co-chairperson," said Ms. Callahan. "There's still a lot of work to be done."

"But I'll have it tomorrow," Oliver protested. "I just got a little behind."

"All right," said Ms. Callahan. "But no more excuses after this."

Oliver sat quietly by himself during lunch. He felt as if everyone in class were talking about him. "Hey, where were you?" Josh said.

"I was busy," Oliver replied angrily.

Josh lifted his hands and stepped back. "Sorry," he said. "I was only asking."

Oliver watched Rusty head for his table. "Now I'm finished," he thought.

Rusty put down his tray and smiled a sinister smile. "Mind if I have a word with you, pal?" he said.

"No," said Oliver.

Rusty stared at Josh. "This is private," he said. "Scram."

Josh left.

"I bet you're wondering what I've got up my sleeve," Rusty grinned.

Knowing Rusty, Oliver was sure it *wasn't* something he'd like.

"Look, Rusty," Oliver said, "that camel is Arabella's pet. It means a lot to her."

"Keeping a camel is illegal," said Rusty. "I

could call the Humane Society and have her reported." Rusty paused. "But I have a better idea."

"What?" said Oliver cautiously.

"Simple," said Rusty. "I hear you're having some trouble keeping up with your duties as chairperson. If you appoint me co-chairperson, I promise not to tell anyone about the camel you're baby-sitting."

Oliver was speechless. Rusty as co-chairperson?

Just then Sam walked up. "Hey, did you hear the news?" Rusty said. "Oliver has just appointed me co-chairperson of the Harvest Fair."

Sam looked at Oliver and blinked. "Is that true?" Sam said. Oliver nodded grimly.

"Well," said Rusty, "aren't you going to congratulate me?" He slapped Oliver on the back. "Oliver and I are calling a special meeting for this afternoon at three o'clock. Isn't that right, Oliver, old pal?"

CHAPTER
4

Rusty banged his fist on the table. "This meeting will now come to order," he said. He looked around the table and grinned. "Would someone tell me what activities we have planned this year?"

"The same as usual," Josh scowled. "A hayride, apple bobbing, games—"

"Ah-ha!" interrupted Rusty. "Just what I thought. The same boring stuff."

The Harvest Fair committee members stirred in their chairs.

"I'd like to make some changes," Rusty said. "First, I think we should have a dirt-bike course instead of the hayride."

"But we've already ordered the hayride," Oliver protested.

"Quiet," said Rusty. "I have the floor." He continued with a flourish. "And instead of

apple bobbing, we should have a pie-throwing contest."

"Yuck," said Jennifer.

"I also want to serve soda and hero sandwiches instead of sissy cider and doughnuts."

"But we *always* have cider and doughnuts," said Kim.

"So what?" said Rusty.

"Wait a minute, Rusty," said Sam. "You can't make all those changes without our permission. This is a committee."

"But I'm allowed to make a few suggestions." He slapped Oliver on the back again. "Right, pal?"

Oliver sunk farther into his chair.

"And another thing," Rusty said. "I hated that magician we had last year. I vote for a rock band."

Jennifer jumped out of her seat. "I agree!" she said. "It's so much more adult."

Josh and Matthew grimaced.

"Why don't we take a vote?" suggested Oliver.

Rusty looked around the table. "Not until the other committee members are here," he said.

"What members?" said Oliver.

"I've appointed Jay Goodman and Paul Patterson to the committee," Rusty said. "It can't be only *your* friends on this committee."

Everyone at the table glared at Oliver. "Why don't we adjourn for the day?" Oliver sighed. "We'll meet again tomorrow morning."

"Good idea," said Rusty. He drummed the table top. "This meeting is now over."

After Rusty left, Josh turned to Oliver. "You must be crazy," he said. "What made you pick Rusty as co-chairperson?"

Oliver shrugged. "I thought he might have some good ideas," he said.

"Some good ideas," mocked Sam. "Hah!"

"Yeah," agreed Matthew. "The Harvest Fair is going to be ruined."

"Especially since Jay and Paul are on the committee, too," said Kim.

"I think Jay's kind of cute," said Jennifer.

Everyone stared at her.

"Well," sighed Oliver, "there's nothing I can do about it now." He got up and walked away from the table as fast as he could.

Oliver headed for Arabella's on the way home. "It's not fair," he thought as he rode his bike along. "If Cousin Henry had shown up like he was supposed to, I would never be in this mess."

Oliver pulled up to the gate. "Terrific," he said. "The gate is open again."

He walked into the empty yard. "Okay, Rusty," he shouted. "I know you're in here. What do you want this time?"

There was no answer.

"Quit playing games," Oliver said angrily.

He looked over at the garage door. It was wide open. Oliver suddenly panicked.

"Houdini!" he cried. "Where are you?"

He ran over to the stall and looked inside. It was empty.

Oliver's thoughts raced. "Maybe Cousin Henry

is here," he said. He let himself into Arabella's house. Everything looked the same.

Oliver went back outside. "Houdini!" he called. "Dinnertime!"

He went over to examine the gate. "I bet Rusty did this," Oliver grumbled. But the locks were still attached to the front of the gate. Oliver shut the door. On the back of the gate were lots of heavy hoof marks. The inside latch looked as if it had been chewed off.

Oliver slowly pieced things together. "It wasn't Rusty at all," he said. "Houdini must have pried the garage door open from the bottom. Then he walked over to the gate and chewed and kicked his way out."

Oliver looked at the ground. He could see hoof marks leading down the drive. "Oh, boy," he said. "No wonder Arabella named him Houdini. Houdini was the world's greatest escape artist."

Oliver searched for Houdini until dark. "It's no use," he thought. Oliver returned to Arabella's yard and left the gate slightly open. "Maybe Houdini will get hungry and come back for some food," Oliver thought. He scattered some extra hay around the yard and left.

"Where have you been?" asked Mrs. Moffitt. "I was beginning to worry about you. It's almost dinnertime."

"Sorry, Mom," said Oliver. "I was at Sam's house."

Mrs. Moffitt and Pom-pom were sitting on

the couch watching TV. Suddenly Mrs. Moffitt leaned forward and turned up the volume. "Did you hear this crazy story?" she said.

Kathy Kellogg, the local newscaster, was speaking. "Local residents thought they were seeing things this afternoon when a camel was sighted walking through their back yards. Mr. George Basset of Vanderbilt Drive claimed that the camel ate several of his prize rosebushes.

"Zoo officials confirm that there are no camels missing from the city zoo. They disagree, however, on how such an animal could have appeared in the area. Some speculate it was being kept illegally as a pet. Zoo officials are offering a substantial reward for its capture."

Oliver sank down on the couch and moaned.

"Are you all right?" asked Mrs. Moffitt.

Oliver nodded. How was he ever going to get out of this one!

Everyone was talking about the mysterious camel the next day at school.

"It's probably a joke," Josh said.

"No way," replied Matthew. "There are witnesses who have really seen it."

"The poor little camel," said Jennifer. "Maybe it wandered over here from the Arabian desert."

"Only if it was a good swimmer and made it all the way across the Atlantic," said Sam. Everyone started to laugh.

Sam turned to Oliver. "What do you think?" she said. "You're the pet-care expert."

"Uh, I don't know," Oliver replied. "The whole thing seems pretty hard to believe."

Rusty, Jay, and Paul walked up.

"Did you hear that crazy camel story?" Rusty said. He slapped Oliver on the back. "Ha-ha," he said loudly. "Why would anyone around here have a camel? Huh, Henry?"

He poked Oliver in the ribs.

"Stop it, Rusty," Oliver scowled.

Rusty looked at everyone and smiled. "How's the Harvest Fair committee today?" he said.

"Okay," replied Josh.

"Me and the boys are ready to start the meeting," Rusty said. Jay and Paul shuffled their feet and nodded.

No one said anything.

"Well, I guess we'll begin," Rusty continued. He sat down at the nearest table. "Everyone have a seat," he demanded. He waited until the group was settled. "All in favor of the dirt-bike course raise your hands." Only Jay and Paul voted in favor. "What's the matter with you guys?" shouted Rusty. "A dirt-bike course is a great idea."

The table was quiet.

"What about the pie-throwing contest?" Rusty continued. "Are any of you creeps voting for that?"

Josh folded his arms and looked out the window.

"No fair!" Rusty said. "As co-chairperson I say you have to do some of the things *I* want."

"How about refreshments?" Oliver said politely. "I'd be willing to have soda and sandwiches if we also have cider and doughnuts."

The rest of the group nodded in agreement.

"Sissies," scoffed Rusty. "I bet you won't like my other idea either."

"What's that?" said Josh.

Rusty smiled. "Mumblety-peg," he said.

"But knife-throwing games are illegal," said Matthew.

"Look," said Rusty, "will we do one of my ideas or not?"

Everyone squirmed.

"Well, Kim and I vote for a rock band," said Jennifer, breaking the silence.

Josh and Matthew started to protest.

"Quiet," said Rusty. "You're outvoted." He stood up. "This meeting is now adjourned." Rusty turned to go and then suddenly spun around. "By the way," he added, "me and the boys plan to do some searching for that camel. Does anyone want to join us? I heard they're offering a big reward."

"You creep," Oliver muttered. He was sick of Rusty trying to walk all over him.

Rusty was almost out the door. "Hey, Rusty," Oliver shouted. "I wouldn't count on finding that camel if I were you."

"Why not?" said Rusty.

Josh stood up angrily. "Because *we're* going to find it first!" he said.

Oliver looked at him in surprise.

Sam nodded. "That's right," she said. "We've been planning it since last night."

"Okay, look for it," Rusty sneered. "But don't be surprised if *we* find it first." He looked directly at Oliver. "Maybe I know something you don't know." He turned quickly and left.

"Oliver," said Sam, "will you help us?"

"I guess so," Oliver replied. He still couldn't believe this was happening.

"I'd like to get even with Rusty," said Josh.

"Me, too," said Sam. She smiled at her friends. "Can we count on you, Jennifer, and Kim?"

Jennifer sighed. "Are camels dangerous?" she asked.

"Naw," said Josh.

Jennifer tossed her hair back. "Well, then I suppose I'll help you," she said.

"Good," said Sam. "I hereby name this group the Bartlett Woods Camel Corps. We start searching tonight!"

The first thing Oliver did when he got home was turn on the TV. "More alleged sightings today on that mysterious camel," said Kathy Kellogg. "Zoo officials tried several times to capture the animal, who was reportedly last seen in Arrowhead Park. So far the camel has managed to evade all searchers."

Oliver breathed a sigh of relief. Maybe he and his friends could find Houdini first.

Oliver called Sam. "Did you listen to the news?"

"Yes," she replied. "Why don't we all meet in Arrowhead Park?"

"Good idea," said Oliver. "I'll be at the playground right after I walk Pom-pom."

*   *   *

56

Oliver was the last to arrive at the playground.

"Where do we start?" asked Matthew.

"The first thing we need to do is find some camel tracks," Oliver told him. He used a stick to draw a picture in the dirt. "This is what we're looking for . . . large, two-toed hooves."

"Are they really that big?" asked Jennifer.

Oliver nodded.

"Why don't we split up into three groups?" suggested Josh. "We can cover more territory."

"Good idea," said Oliver. "We have only about an hour of daylight left."

Several minutes later Oliver heard a shout near the jungle gym. "We've found some prints!" Josh and Sam yelled. Everyone ran over. There were four large hoofprints.

"Come on," Oliver said. "It looks like they lead toward the duck pond."

Jennifer grabbed Oliver's arm. "Are you sure this is safe?" she said.

"Don't be such a chicken," Josh said.

But there was nothing at the water's edge except a few ducks.

"Now what?" said Kim.

"I can't find any more tracks," Oliver sighed.

"I don't understand," said Sam. "How can a camel be so difficult to find?"

"He must have waded through the pond and come out on the other side by the cement sidewalk," Oliver answered. "We can't follow his tracks across cement." Oliver thought hard. Where else would Houdini go? "The rose garden!" he said suddenly. "Let's try the rose garden. Camels love to eat thorns."

"It's worth a try," said Sam. "Let's go!"

The rose garden looked eerie in the twilight. It covered almost an acre of land and had a small wooden shelter, or gazebo, in the middle. The Camel Corps moved along the gravel path in a slow cluster.

"Look!" Kim pointed. "Over by the gazebo."

About fifty yards away Houdini stood munching on a large rosebush.

"It's him!" said Oliver.

The cluster got tighter.

"He's bigger than I expected," said Jennifer.

"I've never seen a real camel," added Kim.

"We've got to move very quietly or we'll startle him," Oliver whispered. "Camels are easily frightened." He reached into his pocket and pulled out some jellybeans. "Let's surround him as quickly as possible. Then I'll grab his halter."

"What's a halter?" Matthew whispered.

"It's like a collar," Sam explained.

The group moved forward slowly. They'd almost reached the gazebo when three shadowy figures appeared on the other side. "Gee-haw," shouted one of them. He pulled out a slingshot and fired at the camel.

"It's Rusty!" Josh exclaimed.

"Okay, boys," shouted Rusty. "Get that camel!"

Jay and Paul ran forward and tried to lasso Houdini's neck with a rope. Houdini reared up on his hind legs.

Oliver ran forward. "No!" he shouted. "You're scaring him!"

Rusty spun around. "What are you doing here?" he said.

Oliver tried to grab Rusty's slingshot. "You'll hurt him!" he shouted.

Next to the gazebo Matthew, Sam, and Josh struggled to pull the rope away from Jay and Paul. Meanwhile, Jennifer and Kim tried to throw their jackets around Houdini's neck.

Rusty pushed Oliver to the ground. "Leave me alone," Rusty said.

In one second Oliver was back on his feet. He pulled at Rusty's shirt and started punching him. "You're ruining everything," he said. "What do you know about camels?"

Rusty just laughed. He pointed toward Houdini, who had run off in a cloud of dust. "Too late, pal," he said. "Looks like we both lost this time."

CHAPTER
5

Oliver had never felt so discouraged.

"Now what?" panted Josh. "Should we try to chase him?"

Oliver shook his head. "He's too scared now. We'd never catch him." He looked over at Rusty. "I hope you're happy," he said.

Rusty just shrugged. "Those are the breaks, pal," he said. "See you tomorrow at school."

The Camel Corps trudged slowly home. "We almost had him," said Sam.

"It's all Rusty's fault for scaring him," Josh added.

Jennifer sniffed her jacket. "Yuck," she said. "I smell like a camel."

Oliver stopped at the corner. "You guys go on," he said. "I want to walk by myself for a while."

Oliver waited until everyone was out of sight.

Then he turned up Vanderbilt Drive. "Maybe Houdini had the sense to go home," Oliver thought. "It's worth a try."

Oliver slipped quietly into Arabella's yard. "Houdini," he called softly. "Are you here?"

In the moonlight he could see that the garage door was still open. As he turned to leave, Oliver noticed a light coming from Arabella's house. He walked over to the back door and peeked inside.

A large man with a handlebar mustache sat slumped over the kitchen table. He was snoring loudly. Next to him was a half-eaten plate of baked beans and toast.

Oliver banged on the door. "Cousin Henry!" he yelled. "Is that you?"

Cousin Henry woke with a start. "Who's banging on the door?" he shouted.

"It's Oliver Moffitt," Oliver said. "I'm taking care of Houdini."

Cousin Henry got up and opened the door. "Then where in the blazes is he?" he said.

Oliver gulped. "I don't know, sir," he replied. "He's escaped."

"Ah-ha!" said Cousin Henry. "I'm not surprised. He's just like his mum, that one. I don't know how many times Arabella had to go looking for Genie."

Cousin Henry looked at Oliver and smiled. He was over six feet tall and had on short pants and dark shoes and socks.

"You must be worried to death," he said.

"Why don't you come in and tell me what's happened."

Oliver looked at Cousin Henry suspiciously. "Where have you been?" Oliver asked. "You were supposed to be here days ago."

"Sorry, chap," said Cousin Henry. "Got my schedules mixed up. I thought I was due here today. When I realized my mistake, I tried to ring Arabella, but no one answered. Hope I haven't inconvenienced you."

Oliver sighed. "I'm in big trouble," he said. He explained how Rusty had blackmailed him into being co-chairperson of the Harvest Fair and how the whole town was searching for Houdini.

After Oliver finished talking, Cousin Henry looked at him and shook his head. "Oh, my," he said. "We *do* have a problem, don't we?"

"Are you going to help me?" Oliver said.

"Of course," said Cousin Henry. "Arabella would be mad as a cut snake if we lost Houdini. Besides, the whole thing is partly my fault." Cousin Henry pulled on one side of his mustache. "I'll see if I can round him up tomorrow while you're in school. Give me a ring at three o'clock."

Oliver smiled gratefully. "Thanks, Cousin Henry," he said. "I'm really glad you're here."

Oliver arrived at school bright and early the next morning. The first person he saw was Rusty. "I need five dollars," Rusty said. He stuck out his hand.

"What for?" said Oliver.

"Poker chips," Rusty replied.

"I don't get it," said Oliver.

"Me and the boys thought we'd change all these boring games they do every year," Rusty explained. "Instead of the ring toss we're running a blackjack table and a poker table."

Oliver's eyes grew wide. "Gambling is against the law!" he said.

"Law, schmaw," scoffed Rusty. "Who's going to find out?"

Matthew and Josh walked up. "I bet you guys will want to play," Rusty said.

"Play what?" said Josh.

"Poker and blackjack," replied Rusty.

Josh and Matthew looked at each other.

Rusty stuck out his hand again. "Here's my receipt," he said. "Pay up."

Oliver shuddered. He'd already lost his reputation as a pet-care person. Now he was about to lose his reputation as a chairperson. "I don't have any money on me," he said. "I'll pay you later this afternoon."

Rusty walked away.

"Are you going to give him the money?" Josh asked.

"I don't have much choice," sighed Oliver.

During lunch Jennifer and Kim came running up. "Oliver," said Jennifer, "we have a great idea for the Harvest Fair."

Kim hopped excitedly from one foot to the

other. "We want to rent a camel costume and walk around in it," she blurted out.

"Why?" said Oliver.

"Because everyone is talking about the camel," Jennifer replied patiently. "Besides, it would be fun to wear a costume."

"Do we have it in the budget?" Kim said. "Please? We won't tell anyone. It'll be a surprise."

"I guess so," said Oliver.

Jennifer and Kim jumped up and down again. "Hooray!" they shouted. "Thanks, Oliver." The two girls ran off.

After school Oliver hurried home to call Cousin Henry. "Any luck?" he asked.

"Not a bit," said Cousin Henry. "I can't understand how a camel could disappear."

"The Camel Corps is meeting in half an hour," Oliver said. "Maybe we'll find him."

For the rest of the afternoon the Camel Corps searched.

At five-thirty they called it quits.

"It looks like he's vanished," said Sam. "Not even a single hoofprint."

"Maybe he went back to North Africa," said Jennifer.

"He's got to be here somewhere," said Oliver.

"I agree," said Josh. "Let's meet again tomorrow at the same time."

By the next afternoon it seemed as if the whole town was out looking for the camel. Local citizens walked along carrying butterfly nets, sheets, and ropes. One man had disguised himself as an Arab sheik. Another woman wore a safari outfit.

"Wow," said Sam. "This is better than Halloween."

"The poor camel," said Kim. "No wonder he's hiding."

Oliver was concerned about Houdini's safety. He hoped that wherever he was, he'd stay put.

The Camel Corps gave up around dinnertime. Oliver was baffled. When he got home, he turned on the news.

"Still no word on that missing camel," said Kathy Kellogg. "Some people speculate that the whole thing was a hoax."

Oliver shut off the TV. "Don't worry, Houdini," he said softly. "I'll keep looking until I find you."

On Friday Ms. Callahan met with the Harvest Fair committee for the last time. "Are you ready for the fair tomorrow?" she asked.

Oliver nodded.

"Why don't we go over the activities that you have planned?" said Ms. Callahan.

"We're doing things a little differently this year," Rusty interrupted. "We have some new games—all my ideas, of course."

"I see," said Ms. Callahan. "Why don't you tell me about them?"

Rusty pulled an elaborate diagram out of his pocket. "This is the gym, where we have the games set up," he said. "Usually we have the ring toss here, the apple bobbing by the stage, and the jellybean count on the back wall." He paused and looked around the table. "But this year we want to have poker and blackjack tables right as you enter the room. Any money we collect will go to the school, of course." Rusty pointed to his diagram. "We'll have a mumblety-peg game set up by the tumbling mats, and right outside the door we'll have the pie-throwing contest."

"Hey, we outvoted that!" Oliver said.

"Everyone I spoke to wanted it," Rusty said. "I took a poll."

Ms. Callahan studied the diagram. "I can see you've been very busy," she said.

Rusty beamed. "Great, isn't it? Oh, I forgot to mention the belching contest."

Ms. Callahan raised her eyebrows.

"I've got sixteen kids signed up already," Rusty added.

Ms. Callahan shook her head. "I'm sorry you had to do all this hard work," she said. "But I'm afraid these games aren't acceptable for a school fair."

Rusty leaped out of his chair. "Why not?" he said.

"Gambling and knives are against school rules," Ms. Callahan said. "You should know that. And belching and pie-throwing are in poor taste. I wish you'd spoken to me about this earlier."

Rusty glared at Oliver. "You didn't tell me I had to get Ms. Callahan's approval."

"But I didn't know," Oliver protested.

Rusty shook his fist at Oliver. "It's all your fault," he said. "You planned this deliberately." He got up from the table and stalked away.

Ms. Callahan looked at Oliver. "I'm surprised at you," she said. "You should have known these activities would never be allowed in school."

Oliver breathed a sigh of relief. At least the Harvest Fair wouldn't be ruined. "Sorry," he mumbled. "I guess I wasn't thinking." Oliver stared at Rusty's empty chair and hoped that he wouldn't try to get even again.

After school Oliver got on his bike and rushed home. He turned on the TV to hear what Kathy Kellogg had to say.

"Some new developments on that mysterious camel, who hasn't been seen since Wednesday," Kathy said.

Oliver sat forward in his chair.

"Over at the city zoo animal lovers are picketing against what they call the 'media hype' about the camel. Demonstrator Pearl Florman had this to say . . ."

"That's the Cat Lady!" Oliver exclaimed. The Cat Lady fed all the stray cats in the neighborhood. One time she had helped Oliver look for a cat he'd lost.

"I think everyone should leave the poor camel alone," said Ms. Florman. "I'm sure his rightful owner wants him back." She peered into the camera and lowered her voice. "I happen to know where he's been sleeping each night, but I'm not telling."

Oliver turned off the TV. "I've got to find the Cat Lady," he said. He called Cousin Henry. "Any luck?" he asked.

"No," said Cousin Henry. "How hard can it possibly be to find a camel?"

"I think I have a lead," said Oliver. "I'll be over soon."

Oliver stopped by the Quick Shoppe. "Have you seen the Cat Lady?" he asked Mr. Sanchez, the store's owner.

Mr. Sanchez shook his head. "She was here around noon. Why don't you try the park?"

Oliver rushed off to the park. He spotted the Cat Lady's red wagon a mile away. Then he noticed she was sticking packets of cat food underneath a rosebush.

Oliver screeched to a stop. "Hi!" he shouted.

The Cat Lady jumped. "You startled me," she said.

"Sorry," said Oliver. He paused. "I saw you on TV just now," he said.

"Did you?" said the Cat Lady.

"Do you really know where the camel is sleeping?" asked Oliver.

The Cat Lady pursed her lips. "I should never have said anything," she said. "You're the second young man to bother me."

"You mean someone has already asked you about it?" said Oliver.

"Yes," said the Cat Lady. "That tall boy who always plays with matches and frightens the cats."

"Rusty," Oliver muttered under his breath.

"What do you want with that camel?" said Pearl. "The poor thing just wants to go home."

"But I know where his home is," said Oliver.

"Hmph," said the Cat Lady. "Why should I believe you? You're just a boy."

"Please!" begged Oliver. "If anyone else finds him, he's going to be sent to the zoo or off to North Africa. His owner will be very upset."

The Cat Lady stared at Oliver. "Sorry," she said. "I'm not telling."

Oliver's shoulders dropped. "Okay," he sighed. "I'll just keep looking on my own." He walked away slowly.

"Young man," called the Cat Lady.

Oliver turned around.

"Try the park maintenance shed," she said.

Oliver grinned. "Thanks," he said. "Thanks a lot." He ran to his bike and sped as fast as he could to find Cousin Henry.

Cousin Henry was out in the garage cleaning the stall.

"I know where Houdini's been spending the night," Oliver announced.

Cousin Henry slapped Oliver on the back. "Good show, mate!" he beamed. "Let's go!"

"We'd better wait until dark," Oliver replied. He clapped his hands together. "What perfect timing!" he said. "The Harvest Fair is tomorrow. I'll be glad to get Houdini back home tonight."

"What about the Camel Corps?" asked Cousin Henry.

"We're not meeting tonight," said Oliver. "Everyone has too much to do."

"Why don't you get over here around eight o'clock," said Cousin Henry.

Oliver wasn't usually allowed to be outside after dark. He'd have to figure out a plan. "No problem," he said. "See you later."

Oliver had second and third helpings at dinner that night. "You must be hungry," said Mrs. Moffitt.

"I've been very busy," Oliver said. He yawned as loudly as he could. "I think I'll go to bed early tonight. Tomorrow is a very busy day."

Mrs. Moffitt smiled. "That's a smart thing to do," she said. "Why don't you go on up to your room? Pom-pom and I promise not to disturb you."

"Thanks, Mom," said Oliver. "See you in the morning."

Oliver walked upstairs and shut his bedroom door. He stuffed an extra pillow into his bed to look like a sleeping person. Then he carefully turned out the lights and stepped back into the hall.

Mrs. Moffitt was in the kitchen washing the dishes.

Oliver tiptoed down the stairs and slipped out the front door. "So far, so good," he said to himself.

*   *   *

Cousin Henry was finishing up another plate of baked beans and toast.

"Do you like that stuff?" asked Oliver.

"It's an Aussie favorite," said Cousin Henry. "Would you like to try it?"

Oliver wrinkled his nose. "I don't think so," he said.

Cousin Henry mopped up the last bit of baked beans. "Shall we be off?" he said.

"No problem," said Oliver. "This shouldn't take any time at all."

Arrowhead Park was closed after sundown. Oliver and Cousin Henry made their way quickly to the maintenance sheds on the far side. Several tall bushes and fences hid the sheds from the rest of the park.

"Let's sneak around to the front of the main building," whispered Oliver.

"Right-o," said Cousin Henry.

They crept past a couple of rusty gas pumps and an old tractor. In the main garage sat a black and green bus and a dented pickup truck. A single light bulb burned in the adjoining office.

"Who's in there?" Cousin Henry whispered.

"The night watchman," said Oliver. "Come on. Let's have a look."

The watchman was reading the sports section of the newspaper and chewing on a sandwich. He had a small portable radio next to him. After he finished his sandwich, he stood up and looked at the clock.

"Get down!" Oliver whispered.

The watchman stretched his arms and walked outside. He looked around the yard carefully and then strolled toward the back of the shed.

Oliver motioned for Cousin Henry to follow him.

They slid along the main shed as the watchman turned the corner and pulled out an enormous set of keys. He carefully unlocked a smaller shed and whistled a low cry. Inside the shed something stirred.

Oliver grabbed Cousin Henry's arm. "It's Houdini!" he cried.

CHAPTER
6

The night watchman pulled an apple out of his coat pocket. "Here, boy," he said. Houdini leaned down and rubbed his head on the watchman's arm. The watchman scratched Houdini's chin. "How's my buddy tonight?" he said. "You got enough water?"

Oliver edged a little closer. The floor of the shed had been covered with soft straw. A large steel washtub sat in the corner.

"There's a lot of people still looking for you," the watchman said. He fed Houdini the last bite of the apple. "Don't worry. It'll all blow over soon. They'll never find you here." The watchman used a bucket to refill the water tub. "You be good," he told Houdini. "I'll be back later to check on you."

Oliver and Cousin Henry ducked down as the night watchman closed the door and locked it.

They watched him walk around the corner and climb into the pickup truck.

"We're in luck," whispered Oliver. "He's going to make his rounds. Now's our chance."

Oliver waited until the truck was gone. He tried to turn the knob on the door. "This isn't going to work," he said.

Cousin Henry pointed to a tiny window about six feet up. "If you climb onto my shoulders, can you squeeze through there?" he asked.

Oliver looked up and squinted. "No problem," he said.

Cousin Henry bent down. "Up you go," he said.

The window was dusty and full of cobwebs. It took Oliver a long time to pry it open. "I'm ready," he said finally. He squeezed through the opening and dropped to the ground.

Houdini snorted. "Shhh," said Oliver. "It's just me." Houdini rubbed his nose up and down Oliver's arm.

Oliver walked over to the door. "Cousin Henry," he whispered, "are you there?"

"Bob's your uncle," he replied.

"What?" said Oliver.

"Sorry," said Cousin Henry. "It's an Aussie expression. It means 'everything's okay.' "

"I'm going to try to unlock the door from the inside," Oliver said. He fiddled with the latch for a few minutes. "Perfect," he said. The door opened slowly.

"I'll hold his harness while you hold the door," Oliver whispered.

Cousin Henry nodded.

Oliver led Houdini outside.

"Which way?" said Cousin Henry.

Oliver gestured to the left. As the trio made its way around the shed, a truck could be heard in the distance.

Cousin Henry looked at Oliver. "It's the watchman!" he said. "Hurry!"

Oliver and Cousin Henry tugged on Houdini's halter. "Let's go," Cousin Henry said. Houdini stopped.

Oliver could see the headlights approaching. "Please, Houdini," he said. "This is no time to be stubborn." But Houdini wasn't about to budge.

The pickup truck roared into the maintenance area. "Hey," yelled the night watchman. "What do you think you're doing?" He flipped on his powerful searchlight.

Houdini threw back his head and roared.

Oliver let go quickly. "Uh-oh. Let's get out of here," he said.

Houdini stamped his feet and spun out of control. Oliver and Cousin Henry took off in one direction and Houdini in the other.

The watchman turned on his loudspeaker. "Come back here," he called. He waved his searchlight around the yard, then sped after Oliver and Cousin Henry.

Oliver and Cousin Henry ducked through a hedge and ran across a large field until they were out of breath. "I think we lost him," panted Oliver. He looked over his shoulder and shook his head. "We really blew it. At least Houdini

was safe with the night watchman. Now we don't know where he is."

Cousin Henry nodded. "You're right," he said. "We'll never find him tonight. He's too scared. Our only hope is that he returns home." Cousin Henry patted Oliver's back. "Don't be discouraged, mate," he said. "I'll look for him tomorrow. He'll turn up soon."

"I hope so," Oliver said. "I really hope so."

Oliver tossed and turned for the rest of the night. Tomorrow was the Harvest Fair. He knew he wouldn't have any time to look for Houdini. What if someone else found the camel first? What if Houdini hurt himself?

In the morning Oliver was out of the house before his mother and Pom-pom awoke. He wanted to be the first person to arrive at school. He had a lot to do.

Oliver still felt exhausted from the night before. As he turned into the school yard, he suddenly rubbed his eyes. "I must be seeing things," he said. Oliver pinched himself and walked a little closer. Beside the fifth-grade classroom Houdini was munching on the bales of hay that Mr. O'Brien had left for the hayride.

Oliver glanced at his watch. "Rusty will be here any minute now," he said.

Houdini was too busy eating to notice Oliver sneaking up on him. Oliver grabbed his halter firmly. "Gotcha!" he said. He gave a firm tug, and Houdini lifted his head.

Oliver looked around the playground for a

safe hiding place. "Nothing out here," he said. He tried the classroom door. It was open. He led Houdini into the fifth-grade classroom. "You stay there until I can call Cousin Henry," he said. He closed the door and ran back outside.

Rusty was strolling across the playground. " 'Morning, pal," he said waving. "Ready for the big fair?"

Oliver gulped. "Hi, Rusty," he said.

Rusty stuck out his hand. "I'm sorry I got so mad yesterday," he said. "Let's shake."

Oliver reluctantly took Rusty's hand. A buzzing electric shock went through his palm. "Ouch," he cried.

"Ha-ha! Gotcha!" said Rusty. On the palm of his hand was a small metal disk. "Pretty neat, huh? I bought a bunch of these for door prizes."

Oliver rubbed his hand. "Very funny," he said.

Rusty waved a large paper bag. "Where should I put this stuff? I don't want anyone to steal it."

"Put it in the fifth-grade classroom," Oliver motioned wearily. Then suddenly Oliver snatched the bag from Rusty. "On second thought, why don't you let me do that?" he said. "You can go check on the food supplies in the kitchen."

Rusty gave him a strange look. "If you say so," he said.

Oliver carefully let himself back into the classroom. Houdini was just about to eat a mouthful of chalk. "No!" yelled Oliver. Houdini looked over at Oliver and stopped.

Oliver could hear more voices in the hall. He locked both doors and tried to think.

There was a knock at the door. "Who is it?" said Oliver.

"It's Sam," said the voice. "Why do you have the door locked?"

Oliver's heart was pounding. He opened the door a tiny crack. "Sam, I need your help," he said. He grabbed her wrist and pulled her inside.

"What is it?" said Sam.

Oliver motioned toward Houdini.

"Ohhh," said Sam. "You found him!"

"Shh," said Oliver. "We have to keep him out of sight until his owner can come and get him."

"You know the owner?" said Sam.

Oliver nodded. "Houdini is someone's pet. I promised not to tell anyone about him. I have to get him back to his owner, Sam. Do you think the Camel Corps can help?"

"Of course," said Sam.

"Rusty already suspects something," Oliver added. "As soon as the others get here, try to move Houdini to another room. A big tall man named Cousin Henry will be coming to take him home."

"Got it," said Sam.

Oliver glanced at the clock. "People will be here soon for the fair."

Sam grinned. "No problem, Oliver," she said. "Just leave it to me."

Oliver raced down to the principal's office to phone Cousin Henry.

"I'll be over with the truck as quick as I can," said Cousin Henry.

Oliver went to find Rusty next. Rusty was lying on top of a kitchen counter, eating a hero sandwich.

"What are you doing?" said Oliver.

Rusty sat up. "Just checking out the merchandise."

"There's still a lot to do," Oliver said.

Rusty took another bite of his sandwich. "Take it easy, pal," he said. "I'm just having a little breakfast." He pointed to a large bag of apples. "Want me to take those to the fifth-grade classroom?"

Oliver grabbed the bag. "No!" he said. "I'll do it."

Rusty lay back down. "Whatever you say."

On his way up the hall Oliver met Jennifer and Kim. "Sam needs to talk to you in the fifth-grade classroom," he said.

They both nodded.

"Take these apples," he added. "They're for the apple-bobbing contest."

Oliver stopped by the gym. Everything was still a big mess. Kim and Jennifer were supposed to decorate the stage for the rock band. Jay and Paul had unraveled streamers of crepe paper to hang along the walls. Jay held up a large cutout of a harvest cornucopia. "You sure you want to put this thing up?" he said.

Oliver sighed. "Leave it down if you want," he said.

"Psst," said a voice behind Oliver. He turned around. Sam was motioning to him.

"I left the camel with Kim and Jennifer. We moved him to the first-grade classroom," she whispered. "I'm going to find Matthew and Josh."

"Good," said Oliver. "I'll get the rest of the fair stuff out of the fifth-grade room."

As Oliver sorted through the bags of door prizes and decorations, Rusty suddenly burst through the door. For a moment he stood very still. Then he slowly began to walk around the room.

"What do you want?" said Oliver.

Rusty ran his hand along the chalk tray. "Nothing," he replied. He wandered over and opened the supply closet.

"Are you looking for something?" said Oliver.

"Maybe," said Rusty. He stood in the middle of the room and took a deep breath. "How come it smells funny in here?" he said.

Oliver shrugged. "Beats me," he replied.

Rusty nodded slowly. "I'll be in the gym," he said.

Oliver waited until Rusty walked all the way down the hall. Then he ran to the first-grade classroom and knocked softly on the door. "It's Oliver. Let me in," he said.

Kim opened the door. She looked nervous.

"What's the matter?" said Oliver.

Kim pointed to the bag of apples. Houdini had already eaten half of them, bag and all.

Oliver pushed Houdini's face away. "No," he said. "These were for the fair."

"He doesn't listen to us," said Jennifer.

There were more voices in the hall. Someone tried to open the door. "Who is it?" said Oliver.

"It's Mrs. Fletcher," said the voice. "What are you doing in my classroom?"

Jennifer and Kim quickly grabbed Houdini and pulled him into the coat room.

Oliver threw open the door. "Hi, Mrs. Fletcher," he said. "We're just having a committee meeting in here. It's quieter than our room."

Mrs. Fletcher nodded. "Fine," she said. "Just leave everything where you found it."

Oliver shut the door and ran over to the coat room. Jennifer was desperately trying to pull away as Houdini chewed on the bottom of her sweatshirt.

"Get him off me," Jennifer muttered.

"No, Houdini," said Oliver. He pulled the slimy sweatshirt out of Houdini's mouth.

"I think I'm going to throw up," said Jennifer.

Oliver looked at Kim and Jennifer. "This isn't a good place to hide him. He has to be moved."

"What about the kitchen?" said Kim. "No one is allowed in there."

Oliver peered down the hall. "Let's hurry," he said. "The coast is clear."

Oliver waved an apple in front of Houdini's nose to move him along. "I hope he's safe in here," Oliver said.

"Can we go now?" said Jennifer. Oliver no-

ticed that the bottom of Jennifer's sweatshirt was completely stretched out.

"I'll see if Josh and Matthew are around," he replied.

More people started to arrive. "How am I going to get Houdini out to the truck?" Oliver wondered.

Matthew and Josh rushed up. "Where is he?" said Josh.

"In the kitchen," Oliver replied. He was relieved to see Cousin Henry come around the corner. "Hurry," Oliver said. "Matthew and Josh will help you while I keep track of Rusty."

Oliver met Rusty coming up the hall with the half-eaten bag of apples. "Okay, Moffitt," he said. "Confess. Cousin Henry's around, isn't he?"

"Jennifer and Kim ate those apples," said Oliver. "They both told me they hadn't had any breakfast."

Rusty smirked. "Eight apples and a grocery bag?" he said. "They must have been *really* hungry."

"Where are you going?" said Oliver.

"To the kitchen to get a jar for the jellybean count," Rusty replied. "Why?" A smile of recognition crossed Rusty's face. "Ah-ha!" he said. "I smell a rat." He started to run toward the kitchen.

Oliver grabbed his arm. "Wait," he said.

Rusty pushed him away. "Lay off," he said. Rusty burst through the doors. A half-eaten bag of jellybeans sat on the kitchen counter. "More evidence!" pointed Rusty. He circled the kitchen slowly. "I know he's in here somewhere," he said.

Oliver held his breath as Rusty looked behind every door and under every counter. "Rats," he said finally. "I must have missed him." He shook his fist angrily. "You wait, Moffitt," he said. "He's not going to get away from me again." He stormed out of the kitchen, slamming the door behind him.

Oliver stood quietly for a moment. Then he heard a faint knocking. Oliver pulled open the walk-in refrigerator. "Oh, no," he said.

Josh, Matthew, and Cousin Henry were huddled in the corner. Houdini had his head buried in a lettuce bin. "Good thing you heard us," said Cousin Henry. "We were starting to get a bit chilly."

"We can use the back door to sneak out of here," whispered Oliver. He pushed the door open, peeked around, and gave a sigh of relief. The Harvest Fair was on the other side of the school. Nobody was coming to this side. The whole parking lot was empty—except for Cousin Henry's truck. "Come on," Oliver said.

They dashed across the parking lot with Oliver in the lead. Then the truck's door swung open. Oliver's heart nearly flew out of his chest until he recognized the person in the back of the truck. It was Arabella.

"Surprised you, didn't I?" the Fence Lady said. "Cousin Henry should have told you that I came back early."

Oliver felt himself being pushed from behind. Then Houdini shoved his way past, jumped up into the truck, and began nuzzling Arabella's hands. "You bad boy," Arabella said, patting Houdini's head. "Running away like that and making all this trouble."

She smiled at Oliver. "You did a very good job of finding him. But I'm afraid Houdini is just getting too big to keep behind a fence," she said. "Cousin Henry will take Houdini along with him, and make a stopover in North Africa on his way home. Won't that be nice?" she asked Houdini. "You'll go for an airplane ride."

Turning to Oliver again, Arabella said, "Besides, I ran into Houdini's mother during my trip. She looked very sad without her baby. Now they'll be back together again. I'll just have to get a new pet." She smiled. "Oliver, how are you with bandicoots?"

"Bandicoots?" Oliver repeated.

"Uh, Oliver," Josh whispered. "We'd better be getting back. The fair is supposed to start any second now."

"Right. No problem," Oliver said. "Well, good-bye, Cousin Henry and Houdini." When he heard his name, Houdini turned his head and nodded. "And good luck. I'll miss you!" Oliver ran back into the school with Josh and Matthew.

When they reached the gym, it was full of people. Oliver glanced around the room nervously.

"You've done a wonderful job, Oliver," said Ms. Callahan.

"Thanks," he replied.

There was a loud commotion near the stage. Rusty was waving his arms and hopping up and down. "Look, everyone," he pointed. He grabbed the microphone and climbed up on the stage. "Do you see what I see?"

Behind the curtain Oliver could see a faint silhouette. It had four legs—and a hump. "Oh, no," he muttered. "Houdini must have gotten loose again and wandered up onto the stage."

"I think we just located that mysterious camel," Rusty continued. Oliver held his breath as the curtain went up.

"I found him!" shouted Rusty. "Look!"

The whole crowd started to laugh. "Look, Mommy," pointed a little girl. "It's only a pretend camel."

Rusty spun around. "What are you talking about?" he said.

The crowd began to clap. "Good work," said one person. "A nice surprise," said another.

Oliver watched in disbelief as Kim and Jennifer pranced around the stage in their camel costume.

Mr. Thompson came over and patted Oliver on the back. "Clever idea," he said.

Rusty's ears went red, and he stamped his foot. "No, you don't understand," he shouted. "There really *is* a camel wandering around the school."

One of the teachers shook her head and laughed. "That Rusty certainly is a good actor," she said.

Oliver slipped to the back door of the gym. It was wide open, and he could see Cousin Henry driving by in his truck. The back window suddenly popped open, and a head on a long neck poked out—Houdini! Oliver could see him. Rusty could see him too, since he was facing the back of the gym. But everyone else was looking at the stage.

"There he is! There he *really* is!" Rusty screamed, pointing out the doors. But before the crowd could turn, Houdini's head was hauled back into the truck.

"Knock it off, Rusty," a voice came from the crowd. "This isn't so funny anymore."

Rusty stood frozen, still pointing. "B-b-but . . ." he said.

Cousin Henry leaned out of the truck and gave Oliver a thumbs-up sign. "Bob's your uncle!" he shouted.

"What's that mean?" said Josh.

Oliver smiled. "It's an Australian saying," he said. "It means 'everything has turned out okay.' "